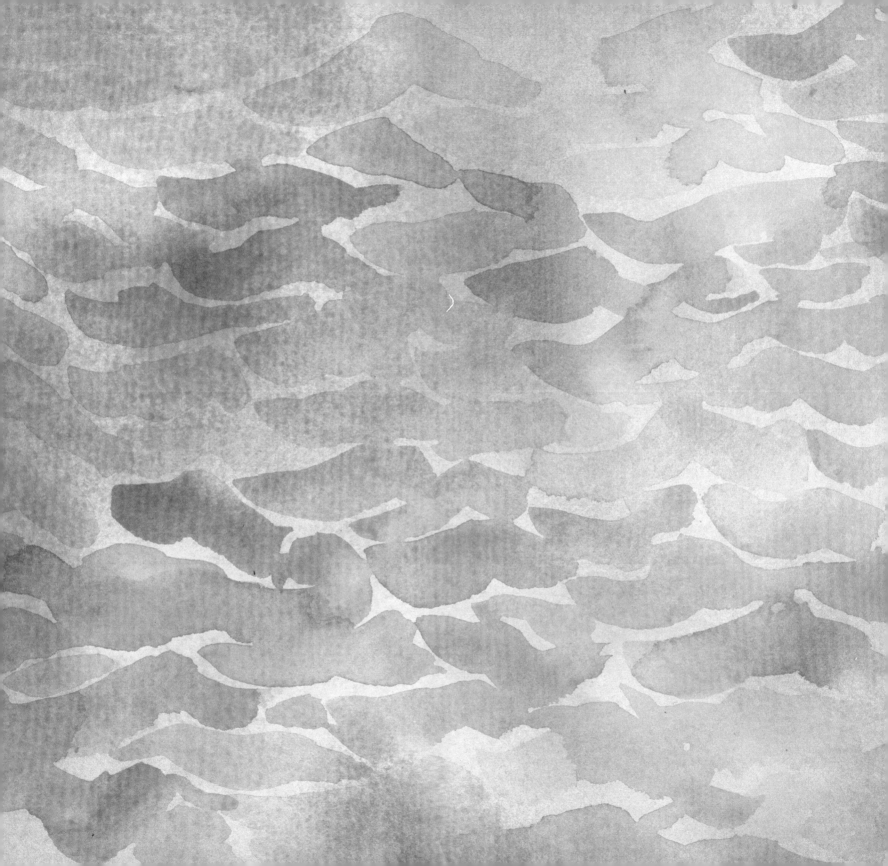

CLEO AND CORNELIUS

A TALE OF TWO CITIES AND TWO KITTIES

By Elizabeth Nicholson, Janine Pibal, and Nick Geller
Illustrated by Michelle Thies

The J. Paul Getty Museum   Los Angeles

Cleo and Cornelius were kitten cousins
who lived in Egypt long ago, when a queen ruled the kingdom
and cats were treated like gods and goddesses.

One day, Cornelius embarked on a journey.

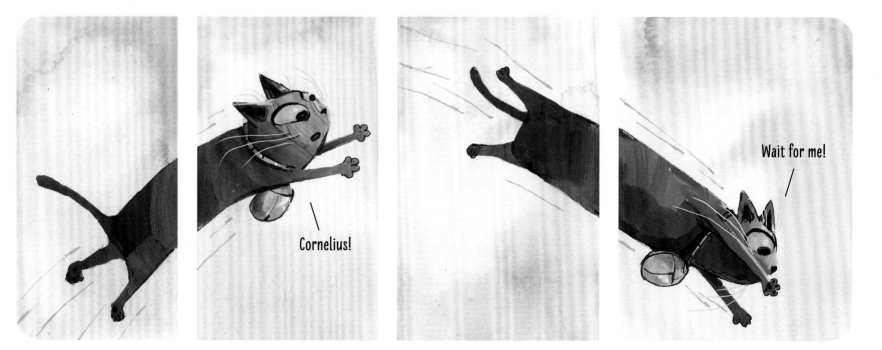

Cleo missed the boat.

ROME

GREECE

CRETE

CYPRUS

MEDITERRANEAN SEA

EGYPT

NILE RIVER

So seasick...
Maybe eating that fish
was a bad idea.

N
W   E
S

Cornelius landed in ancient Rome,
where there were no queens,

dogs were treated like kings,
and cats roamed the streets and
kept mice out of the house.

Cleo waited

and waited

and waited

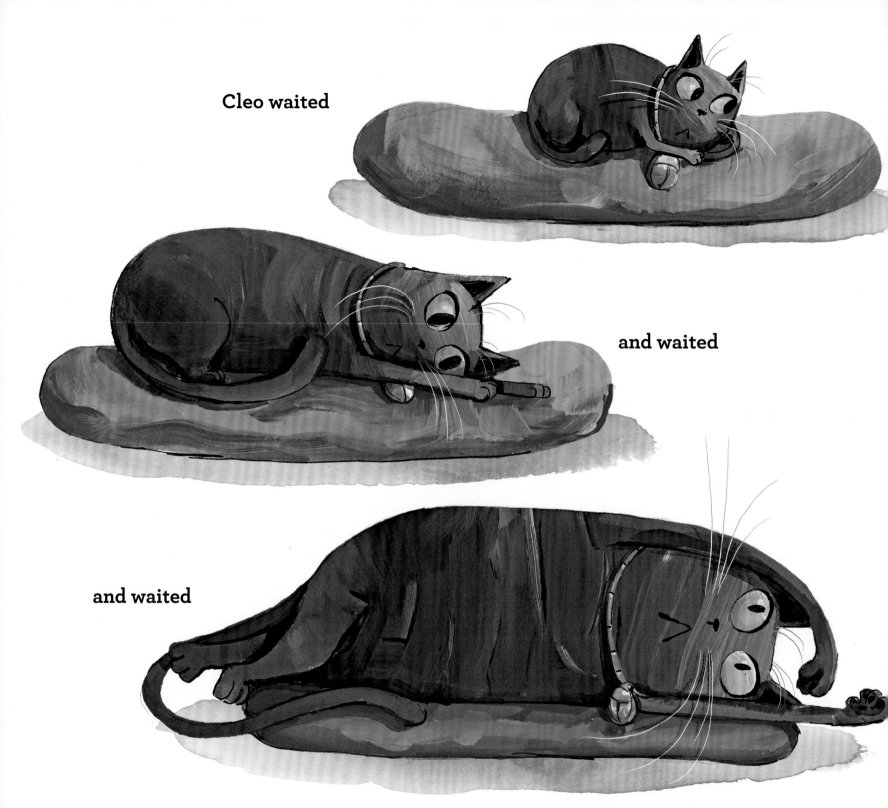

for Cornelius to return.

She missed her cousin
and was bored out of her fur.

Five meals, six naps,
and nothing else to do
for the rest of the day.

Suddenly,
an idea sailed by.

Cleo set out to find Cornelius.

She arrived at
a Roman port.
It smelled spectacular
and felt fabulous.

Cornelius showed Cleo all around Rome.
They pounced and played at a palaestra

and performed in a theater.

One day a country mouse
in his poor home . . .

welcomed his cousin,
a mouse from Rome.

They raced chariots at the Circus Maximus

and dipped their paws in a Roman bath.

How are things back at the palace?

Boring. Nothing to do but eat and nap.

Sounds purrfect!

Their ship was leaving, and Cornelius was ready to go.
The cousins sailed back across the sea.

Goodbye, Rome...

Goodbye, Rome!

They cruised down the Nile, past the
Pyramid of Khufu and the Great Sphinx of Giza.

Look at the giant kitty!

They landed in Egypt just in time
for the festival of Bastet.

Where are all the dogs?

No dogs allowed in the
temple of the cat goddess.

Finally home, Cornelius was content, but his cousin was not.

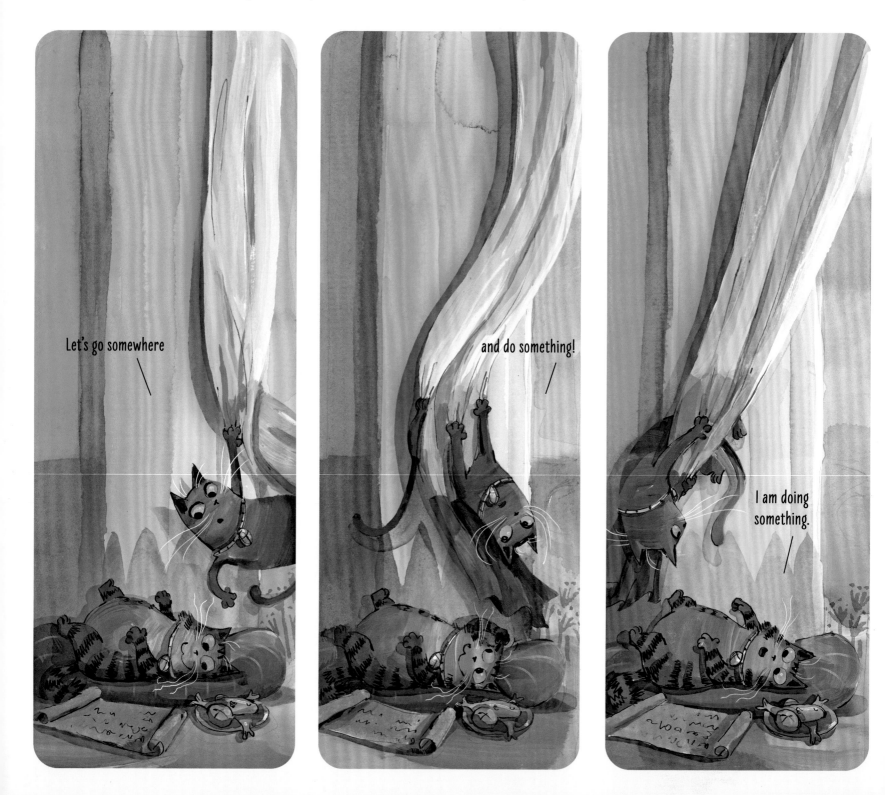

Pampered palace life was not for Cleo. She was born for adventure.

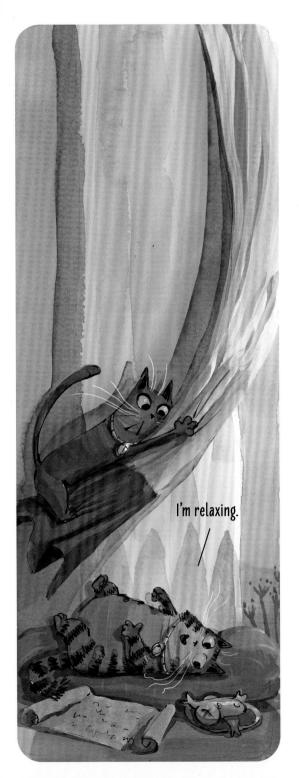

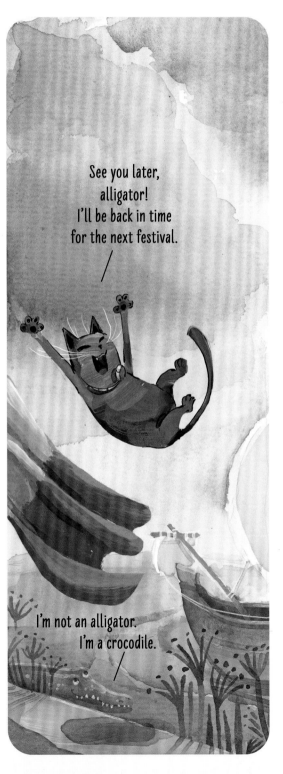

There's no place like home.

Note to the Reader

This book is loosely based on the fable **"The Town Mouse and the Country Mouse,"** originated by the Greek storyteller Aesop in the sixth century BC. The Roman poet Horace wrote a famous new version in the first century BC—around the same time that Cleo and Cornelius's adventure takes place. The fable tells of two mice who are cousins. They visit and show each other around their homes. In the end, each mouse decides that he prefers his own house. But the story of Cleo and Cornelius has a different ending: Cleo decides that she likes exploring new places better than staying home.

Of course, Cleo and Cornelius's tale is fiction, but **cats actually crisscrossed the Mediterranean Sea** in ancient times. In fact, it was due to trade across the vast Roman Empire that cats eventually spread over all of Europe and perhaps as far as China. **Cats were welcome on ships** because they protected the food supply from rats and were believed to control the weather. Sailors considered them good luck!

The earliest evidence of domesticated cats comes from the Mediterranean island of Cyprus nearly ten thousand years ago. **Egyptians started keeping cats as pets around 1500 BC.** By the first century BC, cats were considered sacred in Egyptian society.

They were so beloved that when they died, they were sometimes mummified so they could join their families in the afterlife. Egyptians worshipped numerous gods and goddesses, including a goddess called Bastet, who had a human body and the head of a cat. Bastet was thought of as a protector, especially of women and children. Near the end of their story, Cleo and Cornelius frolic at a festival for Bastet. These festivals were extremely popular, with hundreds of thousands of people attending them every year.

In Egypt, most people and animals lived along the shores of **the Nile River**, which flooded each summer, drenching and fertilizing the soil so that crops could grow. The hippopotamus was the most feared animal of the Nile; it is the strongest creature and has a fierce temper when disturbed. Egypt was also home to crocodiles, monkeys, baboons, and birds such as geese, ducks, and cranes—notice the ibis that sails along with Cleo and Cornelius on their journeys. Ancient people were never far from animals. Disease-carrying rodents as well as poisonous scorpions and snakes were constant dangers. **Cats' skill in hunting** these pests was valued by ancient Egyptians and Romans alike. Romans, however, did not worship cats. They preferred to keep dogs as

MODEL BOAT, 2055–1773 BC
This is a model of a typical Egyptian boat that transported people and goods along the Nile River.

HEDGEHOG, 1877–1786 BC
This Greek-style hedgehog figurine—along with a similar monkey and lion—was found in an ancient Egyptian tomb.

GOLD NECKLACE, 1750–1550 BC
Discovered on the Greek island of Aegina, this necklace combines Egyptian and Greek jewelry styles.

SILVER COIN, 28 BC
With the Roman ruler Octavian on one side and a crocodile symbolizing Egypt on the other, this Roman coin commemorates the defeat of Antony and Cleopatra and the triumph of Rome over Egypt.

pets, but cats roamed wild. They did put food scraps outside their doors, enticing cats to stay nearby and keep mice and rats away. So while they were not treated as pampered pets, **cats were still very welcome in Rome.** Romans used nicknames derived from the Latin word for cat, *feles,* such as Felicula or Felicla, meaning "little cat" or "kitty."

Roman life and lore were full of animals. According to an ancient legend, two abandoned baby boys were discovered by a wolf, who nursed them as her own offspring. Their names were Romulus and Remus, and it was said that when they grew up, they built the city of Rome on the spot where they were nurtured by the wolf. Perhaps this is one reason that ancient Romans favored canines. Dogs were valued as guard animals as well as pets. Sometimes dogs were depicted on tombstones together with their loving owners.

Another well-known Roman story featured birds. Around 390 BC, as Celts from northern Europe attacked, Roman guards were wakened by the loud honking of sacred geese housed in the Temple of Juno. The guards woke up just in time to keep the last Roman fortress from falling to the enemy.

Cleo and Cornelius's tale takes place near the end of **the reign of Cleopatra**, just before the Romans conquered Egypt in 31 BC. At this time, many people, trade goods, and ideas were sailing around the Mediterranean Sea. Some people moved permanently to new countries, bringing along their cultures, religion, and art. One example of such cultural exchange is this very story: Aesop's fable was somehow brought from Greece to Rome, where Horace must have heard it before writing his own version. In another example, the Egyptian goddess Bastet became popular in Greece, where she was associated with Artemis, the goddess of the hunt and the moon.

Cleo and Cornelius was inspired by the exhibition ***Beyond the Nile: Egypt and the Classical World*** at the J. Paul Getty Museum. The exhibition explores artistic and cultural exchange among Egypt, Greece, and Rome from the Bronze Age through the decline of the Roman Empire. It includes almost two hundred rare objects that show the influence of more than one ancient culture. The artworks include statues, obelisks, jewelry, papyri, pottery, coins, and wall paintings called frescoes. Some of these objects appear in the pages of *Cleo and Cornelius.*

Can you find them all?

CAMEO GLASS VESSEL, 25 BC–AD 25
Romans admired Egyptian culture as exotic. This vessel, made by Romans, was decorated with Egyptian gods, pharaohs, and obelisks.

STATUE OF A ROMAN EMPEROR AS PHARAOH, AD 88–89
Statues like this one, made in the Egyptian style, decorated a temple to the Egyptian goddess Isis that was built in a town in the Roman Empire.

OSIRIS CANOPUS, AD 117–138
The head on this jar is that of Osiris, the Egyptian god of the underworld. Yet the jar was discovered in a Roman emperor's villa.

ROMAN MAN AS OSIRIS, after AD 130
This statue of a Roman man named Antinous portrays him as the Egyptian god Osiris. Antinous died during a trip to Egypt, and the statue was made to honor his memory.

Elizabeth Nicholson is senior editor at Getty Publications and former senior writer/editor at the Smithsonian Institution, where she developed exhibition text and publications for all audiences.

Janine Pibal holds an MFA in writing for children and young adults from Vermont College of Fine Arts. She has taught puppeteering for television in Los Angeles. Janine works in the J. Paul Getty Museum Office of the Director.

Nick Geller holds a PhD in classical studies from the University of Michigan. He is a former graduate intern fellow at Getty Publications.

Michelle Thies is an illustrator and background artist for animation. She lives in Los Angeles with her two cats.

©2018 J. Paul Getty Trust

Published by the J. Paul Getty Museum, Los Angeles
Getty Publications
1200 Getty Center Drive, Suite 500
Los Angeles, California 90049-1682
www.getty.edu/publications

Elizabeth Nicholson, *Project Editor*
Amanda Sparrow, *Copy Editor*
Jim Drobka, *Designer*
Michelle Deemer, *Production*

Distributed in North America by ABRAMS

Distributed outside North America by
    Yale University Press, London

Printed and bound in China
    through Asia Pacific Offset (JF17100212)
First printing by the J. Paul Getty Museum (15252)

Library of Congress Cataloging-in-Publication Data

Names: Nicholson, Elizabeth Goldson, author. | Pibal,
    Janine, 1974– author. | Geller, Nick, 1987– author. | Thies,
    Michelle, 1988– illustrator. | J. Paul Getty Museum,
    issuing body.
Title: Cleo and Cornelius : a tale of two cities and two
    kitties / by Elizabeth Nicholson, Janine Pibal, and Nick
    Geller ; illustrated by Michelle Thies.
Other titles: Inspired by: Country mouse and the city
    mouse.
Description: Los Angeles : J. Paul Getty Museum, [2018]
    | Summary: Two kitten cousins leave their home in
    ancient Egypt and travel to Rome in this tale loosely
    based on Aesop's fable, "The Town Mouse and The
    Country Mouse." Inspired by an exhibit at the J. Paul
    Getty Museum, illustrations include hidden objects such
    as a model boat, a scarab, and a gold coin.
Identifiers: LCCN 2017048467 | ISBN 9781947440036
    (hardcover)
Subjects: LCSH: Cats—Egypt—Juvenile fiction. | City
    and town life—Juvenile fiction. | Egypt—Description
    and travel—Juvenile fiction. | CYAC: Cats—Fiction. |
    City and town life—Fiction. | Egypt—History—332–
    30 B.C.—Fiction. | Rome—History—Empire, 30 B.C.–
    284 A.D.—Fiction.
Classification: LCC PZ7.1.N53 Cle 2018 | DDC [E]—dc23
LC record available at https://lccn.loc.gov/2017048467

Note to the Reader photographs, left to right

Model Boat, Art Institute of Chicago, 1894.241. Image: The Art Institute of Chicago / Art Resource, NY; Hedgehog, Oxford, Ashmolean Museum, AN1896-1908 E.3274. Image: © Ashmolean Museum, University of Oxford; Gold Necklace, London, British Museum, 1892,0520.14. Image: © The Trustees of the British Museum / Art Resource, NY; Silver Coin, New York, American Numismatic Society, 1944.100.39163. Image: Courtesy of the American Numismatic Society; Cameo Glass Vessel, Malibu, J. Paul Getty Museum, 85.AF.84. Image: The J. Paul Getty Museum; Statue of a Roman Emperor as Pharaoh, Benevento, Museo del Sannio, 1903. Image: Pio Foglia; Osiris Canopus, The Hague, Royal Collection, 4-1690. Image: Royal Collections, the Netherlands; Roman Man as Osiris, Paris, Musée du Louvre, MR 16. Image: © Musée du Louvre, Dist. RMN-Grand Palais / Photo: Daniel Lebée / Carine Déambrosis / Art Resource, NY